Rr

JAMES

PERCY

MEET ALL THESE FRIENDS IN BUZZ BOOKS:

Thomas the Tank Engine
The Animals of Farthing Wood
Biker Mice from Mars
Winnie-the-Pooh
Fireman Sam
Rupert
Babar

First published in Great Britain 1995 by Buzz Books,
an imprint of Reed Children's Books
Michelin House, 81 Fulham Road, London SW3 6RB
and Auckland, Melbourne, Singapore and Toronto

Copyright © 1995 William Heinemann Ltd
All publishing rights: William Heinemann Ltd. All television and
merchandising rights licensed by William Heinemann Ltd
to Britt Allcroft (Thomas) Ltd exclusively, worldwide.

Photographs copyright © 1992 Britt Allcroft (Thomas) Ltd
Photographs by David Mitton and Terry Permane for Britt Allcroft's
production of Thomas the Tank Engine and Friends

ISBN 1 855 91494 8

Printed in Italy by Olivotto

DUCK AND THE REGATTA

buzz books

Percy and Duck like working at the harbour by the sea.

On a clear summer's night, there is no better place to be.

The big ships bring passengers, and cargo ships carry machinery and other things.

Duck and Percy puff backwards and forwards with the crates of cargo as they are loaded and unloaded by the quayside.

One morning, Duck and Percy noticed that the horizon was packed with sails flapping against the blue sky.

"I wish I could sail to faraway lands," sighed Duck.

"Engines can't go sailing," snorted Percy,
"because engines can't float."
Duck still had his dreams.

Suddenly they were rudely interrupted.

"Wakey, wakey," hovered Harold.

"I'm looking at the boats," replied Duck.

"That's the Regatta," whirred Harold.
"Lots of boats, lots of races, great fun.
I hover around in case I'm needed."

"Do you go to the horizon?" asked Duck.

"Yes—and beyond."

"I didn't know there was a 'beyond'," whispered Percy.

"Do you go to other places at sea?"
continued Duck.

"Certainly—I can land on ships you
know—anywhere, anytime. Goodbye."

Duck sighed.

He went on talking about the Regatta all day.

Percy lost patience.

"Well Duck, I'd rather have my wheels on solid ground. Our rails can take us to all the places we could ever wish to see."

"There's an emergency," called Duck's driver. "I'll check with the Harbour Master."

He returned with bad news.

"A man taking part in the Regatta has hurt his hand. We're to take him to the hospital at the next station. Harold's bringing him now. Come on."

"Good to see you again, Duck," whirred Harold as he landed carefully on the platform. The man was gently helped to safety.

"My job is to stay at sea in case of other emergencies, otherwise I would take this gentleman to hospital myself. Must fly. Goodbye."

Duck set off on his journey.

Soon he was steaming well and his
wheels were thundering along the track.

20

When they reached the station, the man thanked everyone and Bertie got ready to take him to the hospital.

"You looked splendid flying along the line Duck," glowed Bertie. "No wonder they call you Great Western."

"Thank you, Bertie."

"Percy's right," he thought to himself.
"Engines are happiest when their wheels
are firmly on the rails."

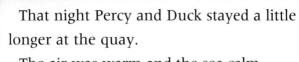

That night Percy and Duck stayed a little longer at the quay.

The air was warm and the sea calm.

"There's a shooting star," said Duck.
"Don't be daft," laughed Percy. "It's Harold—look, he's hovering overhead."

Something fluttered down towards Duck.
His driver caught it.

"It's a flag from the Regatta. Harold's
giving it to you as a present, Duck."

"That was kind of Harold," whispered Duck to Percy. "He may have whirly arms instead of wheels but he seems to understand just what an engine needs."

Duck still wonders about the lands beyond the horizon. But he enjoys being with friends most of all and I think he knows that, sometimes, the best travels are those we can only dream about, don't you?

THOMAS

EDWARD

GORDON